Some more Poeartry

with me 'n' me

AVISHI GURNANI

MBG Publications

Published by MBG Publishing House

Singapore

First published in Singapore in 2022

Title: Some more Poeartry with Me ‘n’ Me

Poetry by Avishi Gurnani

Art by Avishi Gurnani

www.mbg-consults.com

Painting is poetry that is seen

rather than felt, and poetry

is painting that is felt

rather than seen

Leonardo Da Vinci

Acknowledgment

I dedicate this book to my grandparents

who have always been my biggest admirers

and my little brother,

Aarush who is my biggest fan.

I would like to profusely thank my teachers

at New Town Primary School, Singapore

for inspiring and encouraging me constantly.

Contents

Changing seasons

Changing seasons

Swirling as if dreaming drowsily

Swaying as the wind whistles by

Roots stretching splendorously for miles

Lively leaves then falling flamboyantly

Winter on earth dryly descends

Branches creaking, groaning stubbornly

Cold sadness in the air

With a contagious, spreading, infecting flair

Sparing those with a laugh in their heart

Times change as seasons do

Haunting us some of the whiles

Enriching enthralling otherwise

Wilting, drooping till its time again to rise

The clamor

The clamor

The sad clamor
Filling through

Chilling bones

Making one feel alone

That blue clamor

Echoing across

Yonder and beyond

A wounded heart

This miserable clamor

Wanting to be healed

Waiting to be complete

Only but with happiness

Beyond the veil

Beyond the veil

The world below bustling by

Hear them sigh

Wondering

Where is the soul of the night

Light cancelling the shimmer

Pollution blackening the glimmer

Still up there

Beyond this veil

They sail

On the purple carpet of twilight

Like pearls shining in the night

Seek

Seek

A young baby

Fresh inside

Seeking adventure

In the world outside

No inkling of the dangers

Of the perils beside

Make a friend

Follow your dream

Till the day does end

There is joy to spread

You won't regret

Just step right ahead

Undaunted

Undaunted

Wandering around

A sense of foreboding

Held in my heart

Slight sense of danger

A retreat I make

Wrinkling myself

Merge with the petals

Hide in the leaves

Waiting for when

Undaunted I can fly again

Wandering high wandering low

Eager to meet the sky

Eager to glow

Dawn to dusk

Dawn to dusk

Dawn pushing its way

Ready for a new day

From my eyrie

I soar, I rise

Wandering to the farthest skies

Talking to the wind, chatting with the ground

Dusk beckons me to turn around

I am not alone

Amidst every leaf, petal and stone

Carefree, all of them are with me

On my journey

To my eyrie

Mea

Mea

I dream of delight

Freedom to take flight

It's my sun and my moon

The world playing my tune

I yearn for happiness

Promise of a purpose

It's my heaven and my universe

The birds chirping my verse

Beyond any abyss of doom

Ignite to irradiate and illume

It's my star and my sea

All united in my harmony

The tranquil tower

The tranquil tower

Towering tributes,

traversing the tides

Titanics taking-on,

the tenacious torrents

Toiling through,

the treacherous tormenting thunders

Tackling the traitorous tempests,

till tossed thumped thwacked.

Thoughtfully tempering,

the tattered traveler

Triumphing troubles though timorous,

through thrills thick-thin

Testimony to troubled tortuous tenuous times

Timeless tales the tranquil tower treasures

The twain

The twain

A misty breeze spiraling by
Just then a loud sigh
He comes by but alone
Away she has flown
His heart skips a beat
A flutter near his feet
Filled with wonder inside
She perches on his side
With a shake of his head
He offers his hand
And they meet again
With pearly eyes he looks at her
A merry pair back together

Serenity

Serenity

The wind wafting the leaves all around

A serene scene none other can be found

Rays raising spirits

Scurrying squirrels blitz

Mountains standing tall

Hear the burble call

A vivid valley in bloom

An eagle preening its plume

Petals perched with mist

Trees trenched in their midst

The grass swaying so green

The horizon so peacefully pristine

Bridges breaking barriers

Bridges breaking barriers

Bridges breaking barriers

Beaming bees bemused, beckoned by blossoming blooms

Babies beside beastly bisons, bicker blubber babble

Bustling branches bow, barbaric breeze buckling boughs

Bridges bolster belonging

Badgers, bears, boars balancing barefoot

Birds, beavers bungling by birches

Bring bright bubbling bliss

Bridges bending beliefs

Barges banished beyond, brooks binding banks

Bizarre beetles brood, bushes behest battle

Brown boas bearing bonds, bound to baffle

Nature's Alchemist

Nature's Alchemists

Wondering what they whisper away

When they talk, what do they say

A tranquil sanctuary for all to stay

Purifying air every moment of every day.

Providing food and fodder in rife, if used well

Anchoring the Earth and lives on it that dwell

Salving, soothing, sheltering with a spell

Unheeded everything will fail; hear the warning bell

Be selfish we don't mind

But if you cut us down,

No more of us you'll find

Help us survive and we'll both revive

Poeartry by Avishi Gurnani

Titles in the series

Poeartry with me 'n' me

Poeartry with mom 'n' me

Some more Poeartry with me 'n' me

Other books by Avishi Gurnani

Tales in a Tale of a Tail

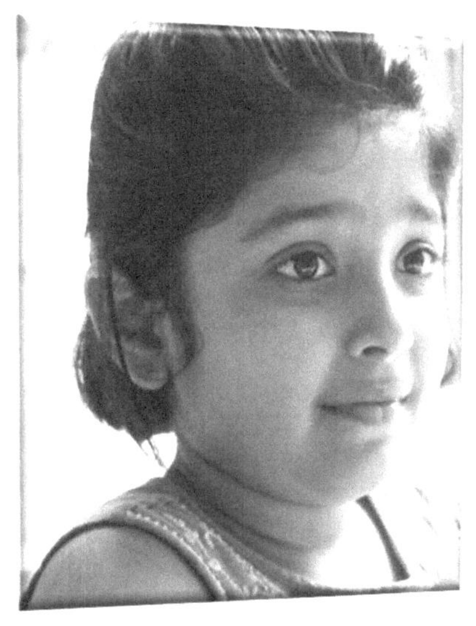

Born in 2010 in India and growing up in Singapore Avishi Gurnani is the author-illustrator of this third book in her poeartry series – where poetry and art come together. She loves to play tennis, piano and spend time with her little brother, the reason she wrote one of her books, Tales in a Tale of a Tale. She feels a deep urge to express her emotions through her writing and convey her ideas.

Poetry and Art come together in this book uniting thoughts and feelings with what I see in my paintings

MBG Publishing House

2022

Compiled and Illustrated by:

Avishi Gurnani

www.ingramcontent.com/pod-product-compliance
Ingram Content Group UK Ltd.
Pitfield, Milton Keynes, MK11 3LW, UK
UKHW061024310726
14090UKWH00023B/82

* 9 7 9 8 4 3 4 2 3 6 0 5 8 *